THIS BOOK BELONGS TO

....

First published 2005 by Walker Books Ltd
87 Vauxhall Walk, London SE11 5HJ

This edition with CD published 2009

2 4 6 8 10 9 7 5 3 1

This book has been typeset in Monotype Bembo

Printed in China

British Library Cataloguing in Publication Data:
a catalogue record for this book is available from the British Library

ISBN 978-1-4063-2095-4

www.walker.co.uk

Mr Large In Charge

Jill Murphy

WALKER BOOKS
AND SUBSIDIARIES
LONDON · BOSTON · SYDNEY · AUCKLAND

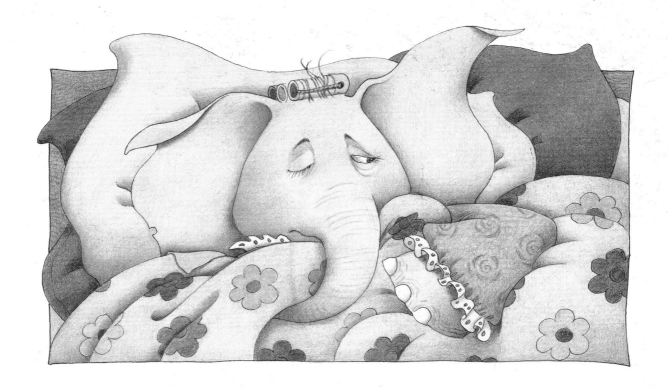

Mrs Large opened one eye and peered out at the morning. She forced open the other eye, dragged herself out of bed and set off downstairs to the kitchen, where Mr Large had kindly started the children on their breakfasts.

"You look ghastly, dear," said Mr Large.

"Don't say that to Mummy!" said Laura indignantly.

"Mummy looks beautiful!" exclaimed Lester.

"Boo'ful Mummy," cooed the baby.

"Yes, of course Mummy's beautiful," said Mr Large.

"I meant she doesn't look *well* – are you feeling
  all right, dear?"

"As a matter of fact,
I *don't* feel too good,"
admitted Mrs Large. "But I was going to take them all
to the park later on. Then there's the shopping and the
lunch and there's–"

"Well, you don't have to worry about any of that,"
said Mr Large. "It's the weekend, so I'm in charge.
Go on, back to bed with you – we'll
take care of everything, won't we, kids?"
"You bet!" yelled Lester.

Mrs Large trudged back upstairs clutching a
nice hot-water bottle and sank back into the
bed, which was still warm.
"What a treat!" she said.

Downstairs, Mr Large was organising his troops.

"Right, men!" he commanded.

"We're not *all* men," said Laura.

"Oh, you know what I mean," said Mr Large.

"Well, troops, then – all right?

I'll take the worst task – that's the washing-up.

"Lester, you can tackle the hoovering – Luke, picking things up off the floor – Laura and the baby, general dusting and cushion-plumping. Quick march. One-two, one-two, off you go."

Mr Large turned on the radio, found a jolly tune to cheer everyone along and soon they were all busy with their tasks.

Upstairs, Mrs Large was jolted back from the brink of
sleep by the astonishing amount of noise blasting up
through the floorboards. She listened anxiously for
a while, but could soon tell they were mostly happy
noises, so she wedged a pillow round her ears and
decided to ignore it.

Mrs Large had just drifted off to sleep when
she was rudely awoken by the baby, who was
giving her a thorough dusting.
"Sorry, Mum!" yelled Laura, rushing in
and grabbing the baby.

The baby began to scream and hung on to
the bedclothes so that they both
fell over backwards.

"This isn't proving very restful, Laura," said Mrs Large
crossly as Laura disentangled herself and the baby, and
attempted to bundle the bedclothes back onto the bed.
"Mummy, huggy!" screamed the baby.
"WANT MY MUMMY! BIG HUGGY NOW!"
Laura stuffed the baby under her arm and wrestled
her out of the door. "Don't worry, Mum," she called
as she closed the door behind them.
"I'll take her down to Dad."
"Don't want Dad,"
bellowed the baby.
"Want Mum!
WANT MY MUMMY!"

Mrs Large rearranged the mangled bedclothes and
snuggled down, feeling decidedly jangled. Suddenly,
there was an almighty crunch from downstairs
and the hoover stopped abruptly.

The bedroom door opened
and Lester looked in.
"It's all right, Mum!" he
reassured her. "Nothing broke,
it just *sounded* bad."
Luke's head appeared round
Lester's knees.
"That's right, Mum!" he agreed.
"Nothing to worry about.
You just go back to sleep –
everything's under control."

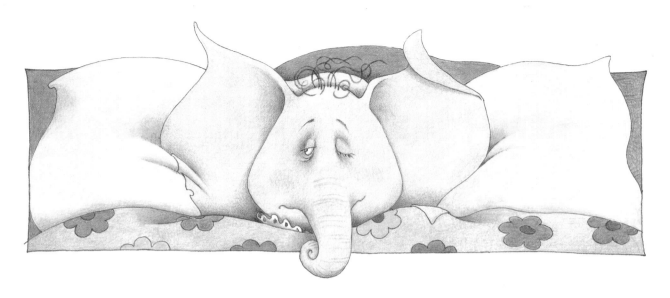

Mrs Large was finally dropping off when Mr Large crashed open the bedroom door.

"We're all off to the park now, dear," he announced. "We'll get the shopping on the way home, then we can bring you up a nice lunch."

"Thank you, dear," said Mrs Large. "I'm having a lovely rest." Mr Large beamed and blew his wife a kiss as he backed out of the room, closing the door *very quietly*.

At last, Mrs Large dozed off. What seemed like five minutes later, she was woken by a smell of burning. Just then, Laura put her head round the door.

"Dad says not to worry about the smell," she said.

"He's getting the lunch and he wants to know if you'd like some."

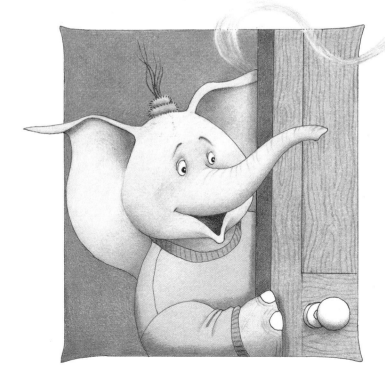

"What exactly *is* it?" asked Mrs Large, nervously.

"Well," said Laura. "It *was* something in a special sauce, but Dad just had a little look at the football on TV – well, it was quite a long look actually. So now it's cheese sandwiches."

"I think I'll carry on sleeping, thank you, dear," said
    Mrs Large. "Perhaps I could join in at teatime."
"Right-o," said Laura, slamming the door as she
    rushed off to tell Dad.

Mrs Large closed her eyes and tried to relax.

What seemed like three seconds later, the door crashed open again and all the children came charging in.

"We're going to play football with Dad!" yelled Lester.

"In the garden!" said Luke.

"Now!" said the baby.

"Are you feeling a *bit* better?" asked Laura.

"Mummy better?" asked the baby. "Big huggy?"

"A *bit* better," said Mrs Large. "You go and have fun with Daddy and perhaps I'll be all right later on."

"Big, BIG huggy!" wept the baby as Lester scooped her up and carried her out. "Big huggy, Mummy. NOW!"

"Don't worry, Mum," said Laura. "She loves football once she gets going!"

The door slammed shut for the hundredth time.
Mrs Large winced and slithered down under the covers.
Joyful sounds came drifting in from the garden
and Mrs Large smiled contentedly.

Five minutes later, Lester burst into the bedroom.

"Dad says where are the bandages?" he yelled.

"– don't worry, Mum, it's not the baby –

Dad tripped over the rake."

"They're on top of the
bathroom cabinet,"
said Mrs Large weakly.

After a while, the door opened again and Mr Large
came in carrying a tray laden with tea and cakes.
The children sneaked in behind him and lurked.
The baby didn't lurk for long. She climbed grimly
onto the bed and clasped her mother round the neck.
"Big huggy," she crooned.

"Everyone out!" ordered Mr Large. "Let Mummy have her rest now. She's not well today." Mrs Large heaved herself into a sitting position and patted the covers. "That's all right, dear," she said. "I've had a *very* restful day and I'm feeling *much* better now. Why don't you all join me for tea?"

"Well, if you're *sure*," said Mr Large, and everyone piled onto the bed to tell Mrs Large all about the day she'd missed.

The End

WALKER BOOKS BY JILL MURPHY

★ THE LAST NOO-NOO

WINNER OF THE SMARTIES BOOK PRIZE, 0–5 YEARS CATEGORY • WINNER OF THE SHEFFIELD CHILDREN'S BOOK AWARD

ALL FOR ONE

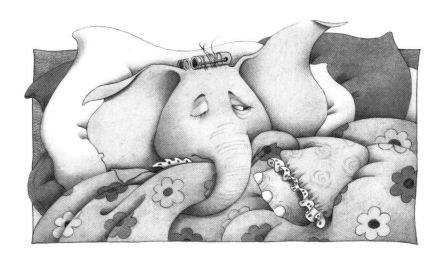

★ ALL IN ONE PIECE

HIGHLY COMMENDED FOR THE KATE GREENAWAY MEDAL

A PIECE OF CAKE • A QUIET NIGHT IN • FIVE MINUTES' PEACE

MR LARGE IN CHARGE • THE LARGE FAMILY COLLECTION